Annie's Shabbat

~ Sarah Marwil Lamstein ~

ILLUSTRATED BY Cecily Lang

Albert Whitman & Company

Morton Grove, Illinois

The Jewish Sabbath, called *Shabbat* (shah-BAHT) in Hebrew, is a joyful holiday that is celebrated every week. It is a day of rest and family, good food and prayer. Shabbat begins at sundown on Friday evening and ends when three stars appear in the sky on Saturday night.

Six days shalt thou labor, and do all the work; but the seventh day is a Sabbath unto the Lord. —Exodus 20: 8-11.

To my mother and father, who kept the Sabbath. —S. M. L.

For my mother and father, who showed me the harmony of humor and responsibility. —C. L.

Sincere thanks to Helene Tuchman, librarian at Temple Emanuel, Newton, Massachusetts, whose graceful intelligence enriched my understanding of Shabbat. —S. M. L.

Library of Congress Cataloging-in-Publication Data

Lamstein, Sarah Marwil, 1943–
Annie's Shabbat / written by Sarah Marwil Lamstein; illustrated by Cecily Lang.
p. cm.
Summary: Shows how Annie and her family celebrate the Jewish Sabbath.
ISBN 0-8075-0376-2
1. Sabbath—Juvenile literature. [1. Sabbath.] I. Lang, Cecily, ill. II. Title. BM685.L29 1997 296.4'1—dc21
96-53607
CIP   AC

The illustrations are made from rice paper which is cut and painted
and glued onto backgrounds of charcoal paper.
The typeface is Stempel Schneidler.
The design is by Scott Piehl.

Contents

1. Are You Ready for Shabbat, Annie?

It is Friday afternoon, and the sun is going down. It's almost time for Shabbat. I can hardly wait.

I have to get ready. As soon as Jonathan finishes his bath, I'll start mine.

Jonathan scoots out of the bathroom wrapped in a towel. His hair is all wet and spiky. "Are you ready for Shabbat, Annie?" he asks with a grin.

"Not yet," I say as I head for the tub.

The bathroom air is warm and steamy. Debra peers in the mirror and brushes her hair. "You can wear my bracelet tonight," she says. "You'll look nice for Shabbat."

After my bath, I put on my flowered dress. The smell of chicken soup floats up to my room.

I see through the window that the sun is lower. It's time to help Mama in the kitchen.

Mama's at the sink slicing pickles. She's wearing the blue dress I love. "Are you ready for Shabbat, Annie?" she asks with a smile.

"Just about," I say and smile back.

I take the wine cups from the cupboard. Pictures of grapes are curled in the silver. I trace the lines with my finger.

Daddy's coming in the back door and hurrying through the kitchen. "Are you ready for Shabbat, Annie?" he asks as he gives me a hug.

"Almost," I say, and hug him back.

I hear his footsteps on the floor above going back and forth, back and forth.

We're nearly ready for Shabbat.

The steam is rising from the soup, the chicken is browning in the oven, and on the counter sits an apple pie.

Suddenly, there is a clatter on the stairs as everyone tumbles down into the dining room.

Mama lights the candles. As she sings the blessing, she covers her eyes. I cover mine, too. I see between my fingers the light from the flames.

The sky is getting darker.

In the living room, Mama settles next to Daddy on the couch. Debra, Jonathan, and I find places all around them. Everyone looks clean and beautiful. The house is finally peaceful.

Mama and Daddy take each other's hands, and we sing the Shabbat songs.

"Lecha dodi...Welcome Bride Sabbath, Queen of the days..."

Daddy blesses Mama, then Debra, then Jonathan, then me. His hand on my head feels like a cozy hat.

"I'm ready for Shabbat!" I say.

2. A Shabbat Feast

In the dining room, Shabbat light is everywhere. The candlesticks gleam brightly, the tablecloth shines whitely, the faces of my family catch the glow.

Daddy raises his wine cup and sings the *Kiddush*.

Vay'hi erev, vay'hi voker: yom ha-shishi.
And it was evening, and it was morning,
the sixth day.

Daddy says God made the world in six days. God made the day and the night, then the heavens, then all the oceans and the earth. God put flowers and trees on the earth, then the sun, the moon, and the stars in the sky. God put fish in the sea, birds in the air, then all the animals and the people on the land. God worked very hard, and on the seventh day God rested.

Mama says that's why we rest on Shabbat.

Daddy pours a sip of wine into my cup, and we sing the blessing. The wine tastes a little sweet.

Now Daddy moves his hands around and around above the challah cover, pretending he's a magician. Then he whisks off the cover, and there are the challahs!

"Hooray!" say Debra and Jonathan.

"Yay!" I say and clap my hands.

The challahs are golden-brown and braided. They look like crowns on their silver tray.

Daddy puts his hand on the challahs, and we say *Hamotzi*, the blessing over the bread.

Daddy takes a taste. "Mmmm," he says and closes his eyes. "A good one."

He says "a good one" every Shabbat. He passes the challah to Mama, then to Debra, Jonathan, and me.

"Mmm," I say and close my eyes. The challah is as soft as cake.

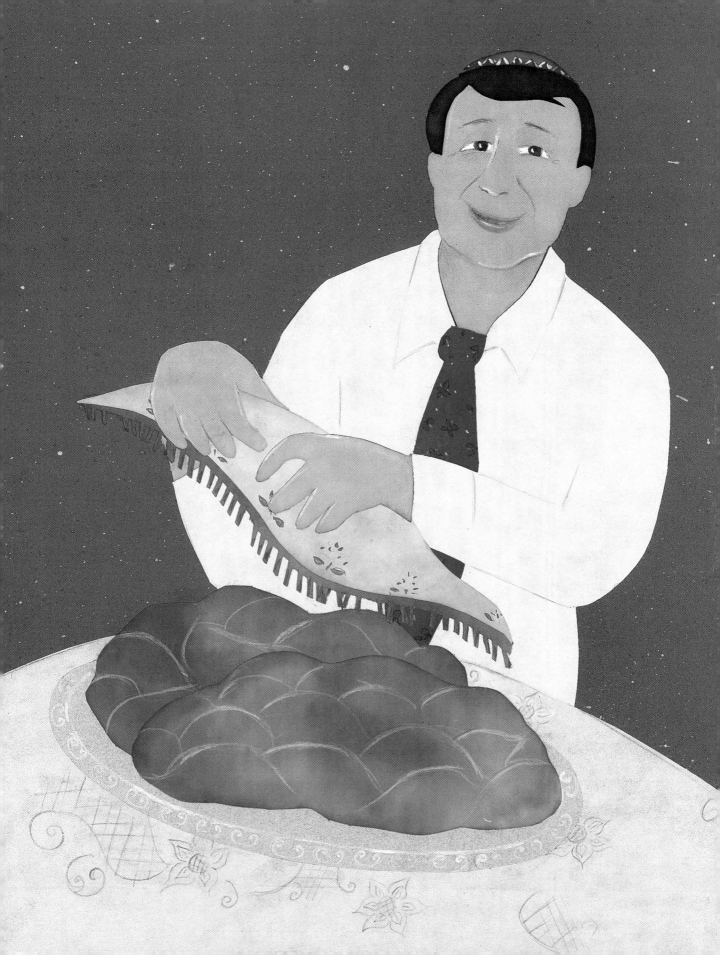

I help Mama with the salad. Jonathan eats my radish. Debra carries in the bowls of soup.

When Mama brings in the chicken, Daddy calls, "The bird!"

I giggle and talk so much that sometimes I forget to eat. But Mama waits for me to finish before she cuts the pie.

It's time to say *Birkat hamazon*, the grace after meals. I hold hands with Mama as we sing the prayers.

Daddy closes his prayer book and looks around the table. "*Shabbat Shalom*," he says with a smile.

"*Shabbat Shalom*," we say, and we smile at each other.

The dining room table is bigger than the one we eat at in the kitchen, and we sit farther apart. But it seems we're sitting closer on Shabbat.

3. Daddy's Story

Saturday morning we walk to the synagogue to say our Shabbat prayers.

I hold one of Daddy's hands, and Jonathan holds the other. Mama walks with Debra arm in arm.

"Tell us a story, Daddy," I say. Daddy always tells a story on our walk to the synagogue. Mama and Debra move in closer. We all want to listen.

Daddy begins. "Wump upon a time...," he says. Daddy always starts like that.

"Wump upon a time, a long, long time ago, before you and me, before Grandma and Grandpa, in fact, more than three thousand years ago, the Jewish people fled the land of Egypt, where they were slaves. Their leader, Moses, led them through the desert to the Promised Land, the land of Canaan.

"The Jewish people had been traveling in the desert only a little while when they began to grumble.

"'Why did we ever leave Egypt?' they muttered to Moses. 'We were slaves there, but at least we had food. Here there is nothing to eat but sand and air.'

"God heard the people grumbling and said to Moses, 'I will cause bread to rain down from the heavens. The people may gather it every morning, enough for one day.'

"The next morning, a white bread lay on the ground above the dew, enough for all the people. They gathered the bread, which they called *manna*, and their stomachs were filled."

"Did the magic bread come every morning?" I ask.

"Every morning," says Daddy. "And on the sixth morning, there was a double portion, enough for Shabbat."

"So the Jewish people could rest on Shabbat?" I ask.

"Yes," says Daddy. "For forty years the Jewish people wandered in the desert, and God gave them manna every day and enough for every Shabbat until they reached the Promised Land."

"I heard that story in Hebrew School," Jonathan says.

"It is a story from the Torah," says Daddy.

"We read the Torah in the synagogue every Shabbat," Debra adds.

"It is a book with many stories of our people," Mama explains.

4. A Book with Many Stories

At the synagogue, everyone says, *"Good Shabbos, good Shabbos."*

Inside the sanctuary, we sit with Grandma and Grandpa. I sit right between them.

Grandma's arms are soft around me. Grandpa holds me in a hug.

I like to play with the silken fringe of Grandpa's *tallit*. It feels like water running through my fingers.

I see Sandy Forman sitting with her sisters, Ruth and Helen. They all have red hair. Sandy winks at me. I wink back twice.

Now everyone is standing. The cantor is bringing the Torah into the congregation. He's singing as he comes.

Mama says everyone wants to touch the Torah to show how much they love it.

I want to touch it, too.

The cantor's singing is getting louder. He's coming closer. Now he's at our row.

Mama puts her prayer book on the Torah. She kisses it where it touched.

I stand next to Mama and try to touch the Torah, but I can't quite reach it. I lean way over. I stretch my arm so far I'm almost sideways.

Now I'm touching it! The Torah's cover feels smooth and cool. Its gold embroidery is beautiful.

I kiss my fingers where they touched.

5. Grandma's Story

After synagogue, Grandma and Grandpa come to our house for lunch.

"Good chicken," Grandpa says as he wipes his shiny chin.

When we finish eating, Grandma says, "Would you like a story, Annie?" I hop up on her lap and lay my cheek against her blouse.

"Wump upon a time...," Grandma begins. "Wump upon a time, a long time ago, before you and me, before *my* grandma and grandpa, in fact, five hundred years ago in a far-off country called Spain, lived a little girl named Raquela."

"How old was she?" I ask.

"She was just your age," says Grandma. "Raquela lived at a time when the Jewish people were in trouble. The king and queen of Spain, King Ferdinand and Queen Isabella, said the Jewish people had to leave the country or stop being Jewish.

"Many people left, carrying only a few possessions with them. Sadly, they said good-bye to their friends and to their beautiful country.

"The ones who stayed in Spain had to stop being Jewish. They couldn't celebrate Hanukkah or Purim or Shabbat."

"Not Shabbat?" I ask.

"No," says Grandma. "But they really didn't stop being Jewish. They just pretended to. They had to be careful, though, because the king and queen had spies everywhere to find out who was still being Jewish.

"Before every Shabbat, Raquela bathed herself and put on a clean dress."

"Just like me," I say.

"Yes," says Grandma. "Then she went into the hall where her family ate dinner. She helped her mama put a clean cloth on the table. Then she went to a wooden cupboard and took out five silver wine cups."

"Just like me!" I say.

"Yes," says Grandma. "Then Raquela and her mama left the hall and went down into the cellar. Raquela's mama carried a small stick with a flame. It was cold and dark in the cellar, and all Raquela could see in the dimness were wooden casks of wine and oil. Raquela's mama lit two wicks floating in a vessel of oil. Then she put her hands over her eyes and whispered the blessing. The burning wicks cast dancing shadows on the cellar walls.

"Raquela felt afraid. She knew her family was in danger. But when she looked at the Shabbat lights, she felt a little less afraid.

"'I will keep your secret,' she said to the dancing flames."

Grandma stops.

"What happened to Raquela?" I ask.

"After a few years," says Grandma, "Raquela and her family had to leave Spain. They went to live in another country where they were less afraid."

"I'm glad we don't have to go down to the cellar to light the Shabbat candles," I say.

"Yes," says Grandma. "We're lucky."

6. Three Stars in the Sky

It is after Shabbat supper, and the sun is going down. We're playing Chinese checkers.

"Your turn, Annie," Jonathan says.

I jump my red marble across his green. Jonathan jumps his marble twice over mine.

"Your turn, Debra," I say.

The light in the living room is growing dim.

Debra gets up and goes to the window. The sky is almost dark. "I see two stars," she says.

Three stars tell us Shabbat is over.

We all get up and go to the window.

Jonathan squints his eyes and scrunches his nose. He's looking for three stars.

"I see three," Jonathan says. "One's just above the treetop in our front yard."

I see three, too.

Just then Mama and Daddy come into the living room.

"Time for *Havdalah*," they say. "Time to say good-bye to Shabbat."

Jonathan holds the Havdalah candle, and Daddy lights it. Mama passes the spice box.

We sniff the cloves and cinnamon. The sweet smell makes us feel better about saying good-bye to Shabbat.

Daddy says the blessings, then he puts out the flame.

"*Shavuah tov, shavuah tov,*" we all sing. "Have a good week."

I stand at the window and look outside. I see more stars in the sky—four, five, and six.

Daddy stands behind me, rumpling up my hair. "Six days of the week," he says, "then again it will be Shabbat."

Shabbat is like a present that we open every week. I'm glad it comes again and again.

Glossary

Shabbat (shah-BAHT) Sabbath, in Hebrew. *Shabbat Shalom* ("Have a peaceful Sabbath") is a popular greeting for the day. Many people also use the Yiddish word *Shabbos* (SHAH-biss). (Yiddish, spoken by the Jews of central and eastern Europe and their emigrant descendants, is a mixture of Hebrew, German, and other languages.)

The Shabbat symbols:

The candles At least two lights are kindled in the home to symbolize the joy and peace of the holiday. Since one is not allowed to light a fire on the Sabbath, one covers one's eyes while saying the blessing so as not to see the candles already lit.

The wine The Shabbat meal begins with the Kiddush (kee-DOOSH or KID-dush), the blessing over the wine.

The challah (KHAH-lah) The traditional braided white bread is served at Shabbat and holiday meals; it is symbolic of good food. There are two challahs on Shabbat to remind us of the double portion of manna God gave the Jewish people in the desert.

Hamotzi (hah-MO-tsi) The blessing over the bread.

Birkat hamazon (bir-KAT hah-mah-ZON) The blessing after the meal.

Daddy's Story "The Manna," —Exodus 16.

Synagogue (SIN-uh-gog) The Jewish house of worship.

Tallit (tah-LEET) The fringed shawl usually worn at morning prayer.

Cantor (CAN-ter) The one who leads the congregation in singing and chanting the prayers.

Torah (toe-RAH or TOE-ruh) The Hebrew Scriptures, a portion of which is read every Shabbat. The Hebrew words are written by hand on a parchment scroll.

Grandma's Story During the fourteenth and fifteenth centuries, the Jews of Spain were forced to leave or convert. Many only pretended to give up their Judaism and practiced their customs and rituals in secret. The Spanish Inquisition, established in 1478 during the reign of King Ferdinand and Queen Isabella, tried to uncover the secret Jews, or Marranos, as they were called. Many fled the country or were tortured and killed.

Hanukkah (khah-noo-KAH or KHAH-noo-kah) The Festival of Lights commemorates the struggle of the Jews against persecution by the Syrian Greeks twenty-one centuries ago.

Purim (POOR-im) This festival marks the deliverance of the Jewish people from extermination at the hands of the Persian king Ahasuerus and his advisor Haman in the late fifth century B.C.E.

Havdalah (hav-DAH-lah) The ceremony that ushers out the Sabbath, marking the separation between light and dark, between Shabbat and the workdays of the week. The spice box contains sweet-smelling spices.

Shavuah tov! (shah-VU-ah TOV) In Hebrew, "Have a good week!"